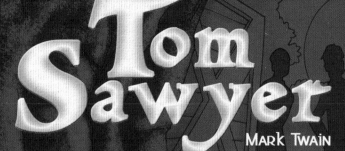

The Adventures Of

# Tom Sawyer

Mark Twain

CAMPFIRE™

KALYANI NAVYUG MEDIA PVT LTD

Sitting around the Campfire, telling the story, were:

| | | |
|---|---|---|
| **Wordsmith** | : | Matt Josdal |
| **Illustrator** | : | Brian Shearer |
| **Colourist** | : | Surya Muduli |
| **Colour Consultant** | : | RC Prakash |
| **Letterer** | : | Bhavnath Chaudhary |
| **Editors** | : | Eman Chowdhary |
| | | Divya Dubey |
| **Research Editor** | : | Pushpanjali Borooah |

**Cover Artists:**

| | | |
|---|---|---|
| **Illustrator** | : | Naresh Kumar |
| **Colourist** | : | RC Prakash |
| **Designer** | : | Manishi Gupta |

Published by Kalyani Navyug Media Pvt Ltd
101 C, Shiv House, Hari Nagar Ashram
New Delhi 110014
India
www.campfire.co.in

ISBN: 978-81-906963-7-1

Printed in India at Tara Art Printers Pvt Ltd.

## About the Author

Samuel Langhorne Clemens, known to most as Mark Twain, has been hailed by many as the father of American Literature. His two most famous works, *The Adventures of Tom Sawyer* (1876) and *The Adventures of Huckleberry Finn* (1884), are considered two of the greatest American novels of all time.

Twain was born in Florida, Missouri on 30th November 1835. He grew up in the town of Hannibal on the Mississippi River, which would eventually serve as the basis for the place where Tom Sawyer and Huckleberry Finn would live.

Twain tried turning his hand to many different professions throughout his life, but continued writing all the while. His first job was as a printer's apprentice and, during this time, he met a famous steamboat captain who convinced him to become a pilot. After two years of training, he acquired his licence and began traversing the mighty Mississippi as the pilot of a steamboat. It was a dangerous and lucrative form of employment.

Twain grew up in Missouri at a time when it was a slave state. After the American Civil War broke out, he became a strong supporter of emancipation, and staunchly believed that the slave trade should be abolished.

Though he began as a comic writer, the tribulations he faced in his personal life perhaps served to turn him into a serious, even pessimistic, writer in his later years. He lost his wife and two daughters, and his ill-fated life never really allowed him to recover. Twain passed away in 1910, but he is still one of the best-loved writers around the world.

5

Well, I don't know. You see, Aunt Polly is very particular about this fence, and only one in a thousand boys could do it just the way it's got to be done.

Oh, come now. Let me just ...y; only just a little. I'd let you, if you were me, Tom.

Ben, I'd like to, but Aunt Polly--

No, Ben. I'm afraid--

I've got it, Tom. I'll be just as careful as you. And, if you let me try, I'll give you the core of my apple.

I'll give you all of it!

Tom gave up the brush with reluctance on his face, but eagerness in his heart. And, while Ben worked and sweated in the sun, Tom munched the apple and planned how to trick more innocents.

There was no lack of material. Boys came along every now and then. They came to jeer, but stayed to whitewash.

Tom traded the next go to Billy Fisher for a kite. And when he finished, Johnny Miller bought in for a dead rat and a string to swing it with. And when the middle of the afternoon came, Tom was literally rolling in wealth.

Tom had discovered a great law of human nature, without knowing it – in order to make a person want something, you only need to make it difficult to attain.

It's not such an empty world, after all.

He had a nice, lazy time. If he hadn't run out of whitewash, he would have bankrupted every boy in the village.

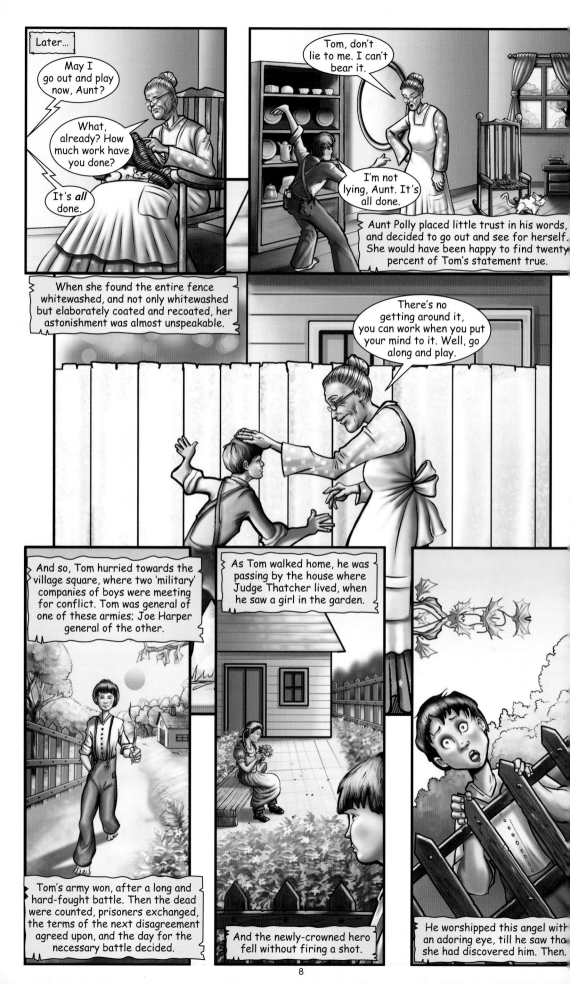

Later...

May I go out and play now, Aunt?

What, already? How much work have you done?

It's *all* done.

Tom, don't lie to me. I can't bear it.

I'm not lying, Aunt. It's all done.

Aunt Polly placed little trust in his words, and decided to go out and see for herself. She would have been happy to find twenty percent of Tom's statement true.

When she found the entire fence whitewashed, and not only whitewashed but elaborately coated and recoated, her astonishment was almost unspeakable.

There's no getting around it, you can work when you put your mind to it. Well, go along and play.

And so, Tom hurried towards the village square, where two 'military' companies of boys were meeting for conflict. Tom was general of one of these armies; Joe Harper general of the other.

As Tom walked home, he was passing by the house where Judge Thatcher lived, when he saw a girl in the garden.

Tom's army won, after a long and hard-fought battle. Then the dead were counted, prisoners exchanged, the terms of the next disagreement agreed upon, and the day for the necessary battle decided.

And the newly-crowned hero fell without firing a shot.

He worshipped this angel with an adoring eye, till he saw that she had discovered him. Then.

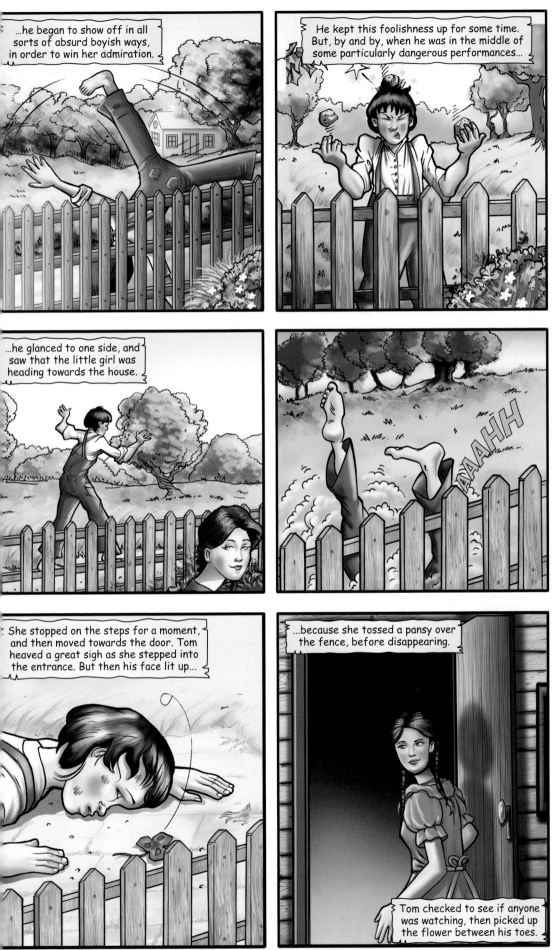

He hopped away with the treasure and disappeared around the corner. Then he buttoned the flower inside his shirt, next to his heart.

He returned and hung about the fence till nightfall, showing off as before.

The girl didn't show herself again, but Tom comforted himself with the hope that she had been watching through a window, and had been aware of his attentions.

On Monday morning, Tom Sawyer felt miserable because it meant the start of another week of suffering at school.

He generally began every Monday wishing he had no days off – they made going back to school so much worse.

If I were to get sick, I could stay home from school.

He checked himself, but found no ailment, so he investigated again.

Hmmm. What was it the doctor said about something that laid a patient up for two or three weeks and almost made him lose a finger?

But Tom did not know the necessary symptoms.

He thought a bit longer, and suddenly discovered something. One of his upper front teeth was loose. He decided to keep the tooth in reserve and go ahead with the sore toe problem.

There. Off to school with you now.

OOOWWWWWW!!

On his way to school, Tom came across the young outcast of the village; the son of the town drunkard.

Hello, Huckleberry Finn!

Hello yourself.

What's that you got?

A dead cat.

Let me see him, Huck.

My, he's pretty stiff. Where did you get him?

Bought him off a boy.

Say, what are dead cats good for, Huck?

Good for? For curing warts, of course!

How do you cure warts with dead cats?

You take your cat and go to the graveyard at about midnight, where somebody wicked has been buried.

And when it's midnight, a devil will come, or maybe two or three, but you can't see them. You can only hear something like the wind, or maybe hear them talk.

And when they are taking the body away, you heave your cat after them and say, 'devil follow corpse, cat follow devil, wart follow cat, I'm done with you.' That will cure any wart.

12

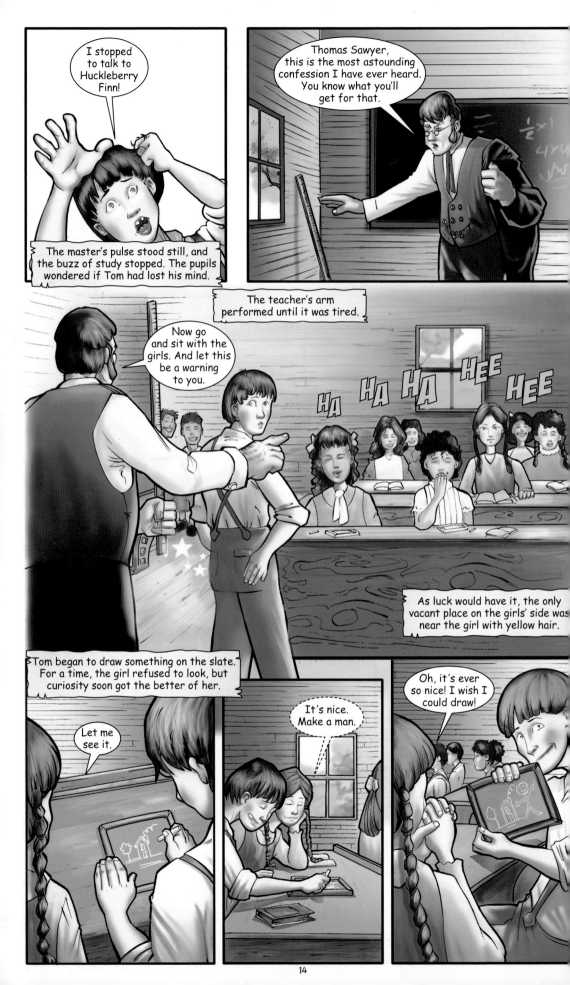

I stopped to talk to Huckleberry Finn!

The master's pulse stood still, and the buzz of study stopped. The pupils wondered if Tom had lost his mind.

Thomas Sawyer, this is the most astounding confession I have ever heard. You know what you'll get for that.

The teacher's arm performed until it was tired.

Now go and sit with the girls. And let this be a warning to you.

HA HA HA HEE HEE

As luck would have it, the only vacant place on the girls' side was near the girl with yellow hair.

Tom began to draw something on the slate. For a time, the girl refused to look, but curiosity soon got the better of her.

Let me see it.

It's nice. Make a man.

Oh, it's ever so nice! I wish I could draw!

It's easy. I'll teach you.

Oh, you will? When?

Sure, at noon. Do you go home for lunch?

I'll stay if you will.

Good. Then I'll stay too. What's your name?

Becky Thatcher. What's yours? Oh, I know. It's Thomas Sawyer.

That's the name they punish me with. I'm Tom when I'm good. You call me Tom, will you?

Yes. What's that there?

Oh, it isn't anything.

Yes, it is.

No, it isn't! You don't want to see.

Yes, I do. Please let me see.

No, I won't – I promise I won't.

You'll tell.

Oh! You don't want to see--

I LOVE YOU

...ecky hit his hand, but ...blushed and looked ...pleased nevertheless.

Oh, you bad thing!

At that moment, Tom was dragged across the room, under a peppering fire of giggles.

Although his ear tingled, his heart was jubilant.

17

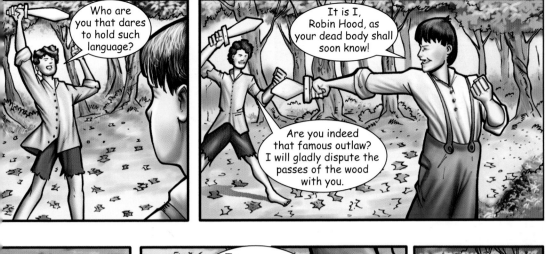

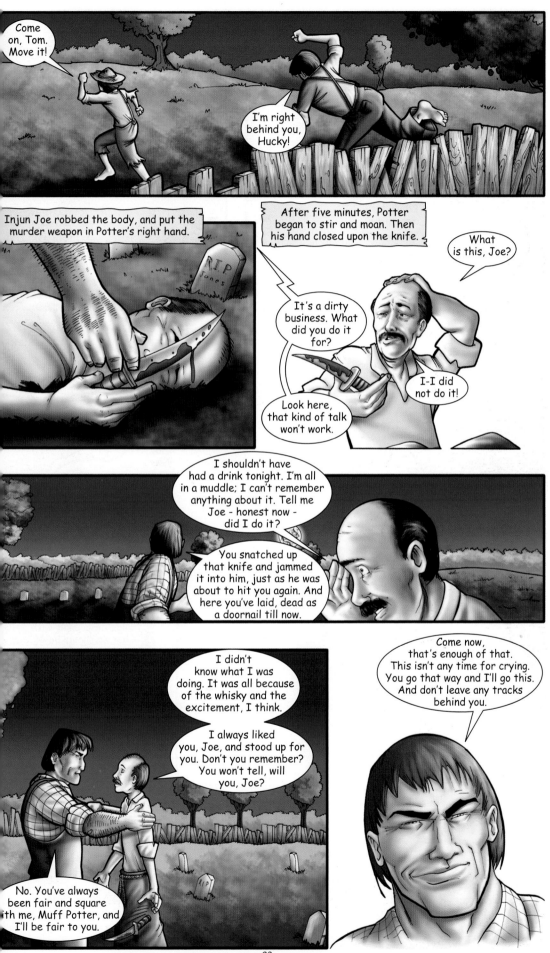

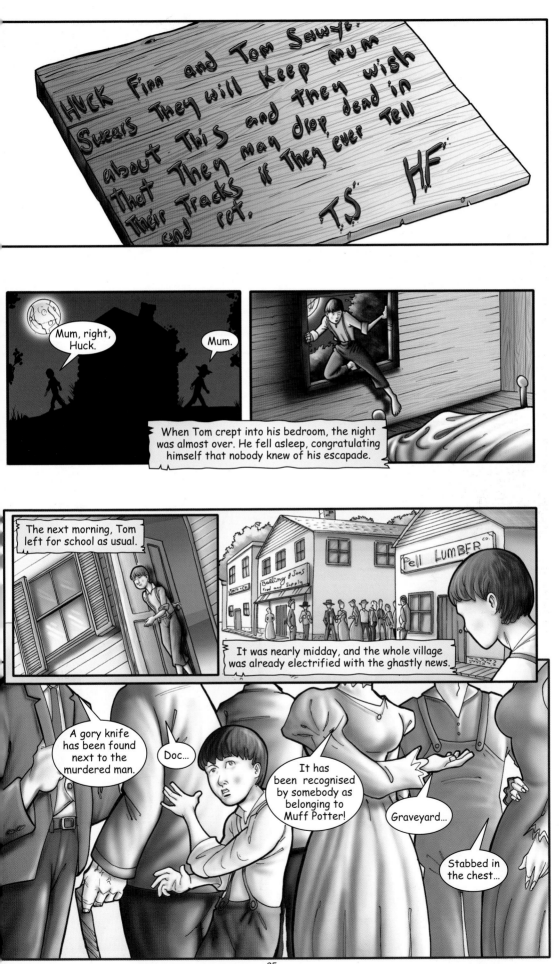

Tom's fearful secret, and gnawing conscience, disturbed him for a week after that.

It seemed to Tom that his schoolmates would never stop holding inquests on dead cats. But he couldn't take his mind off his troubles.

He had no interest in joining his friends, and that was strange.

Every day, during this time of sorrow, Tom went to the little jail window and smuggled as many small luxuries through to the 'murderer' as he could get hold of.

Tom was gloomy and desperate.

I am a lonely, friendless boy, and nobody loves me. They have finally forced me to do it – I will lead a life of crime.

Hmph.

There was no choice.

After school, Tom met his closest comrade, Joe Harper. They were two souls with a single thought.

Why are you so glum, Tom?

That's it, Joe, I'm giving it all up. I'm leaving forever; I'm off to be a pirate.

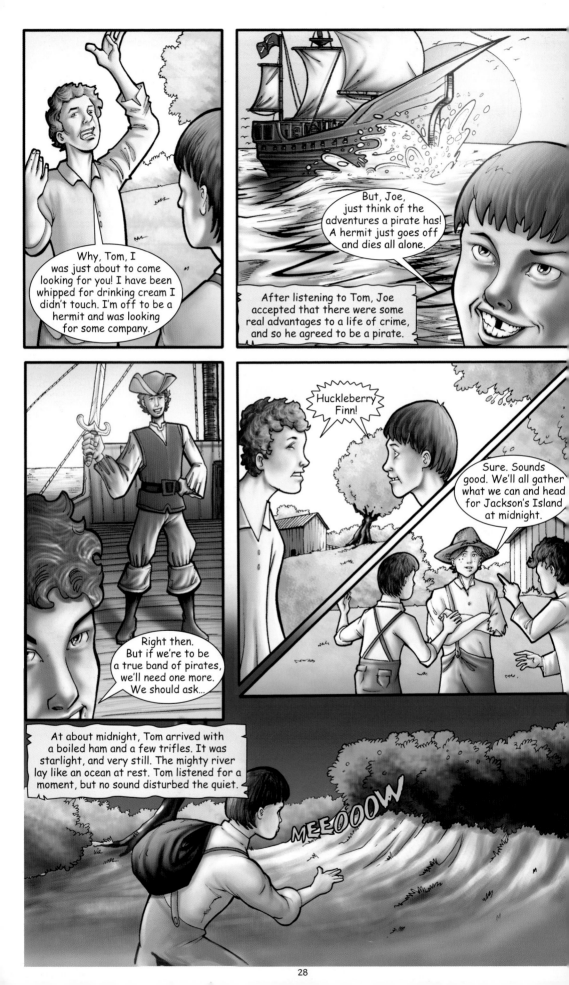

Why, Tom, I was just about to come looking for you! I have been whipped for drinking cream I didn't touch. I'm off to be a hermit and was looking for some company.

But, Joe, just think of the adventures a pirate has! A hermit just goes off and dies all alone.

After listening to Tom, Joe accepted that there were some real advantages to a life of crime, and so he agreed to be a pirate.

Right then. But if we're to be a true band of pirates, we'll need one more. We should ask...

Huckleberry Finn!

Sure. Sounds good. We'll all gather what we can and head for Jackson's Island at midnight.

At about midnight, Tom arrived with a boiled ham and a few trifles. It was starlight, and very still. The mighty river lay like an ocean at rest. Tom listened for a moment, but no sound disturbed the quiet.

MEEOOOW

29

When Tom awoke in the morning, he wondered where he was. He looked around, thought for a while and then remembered.

The marvel of nature waking up and going to work showed itself to Tom.

Yo-ho me lads!

He stirred up the other pirates and they all clattered away with a shout.

In a minute or two, they were stripped and chasing after each other in the shallow, clear water. They felt no longing for the little village sleeping in the distance, beyond the majestic stretch of water.

They found a promising nook in the river bank and threw in their lines. Almost immediately, they got a reward.

They came back to camp wonderfully refreshed, glad-hearted, and ravenous.

For some time, the boys had been aware of a peculiar sound in the distance, but then...

BOOM

What is it?

It isn't thunder!

Soon, however, talk ran slow. The stillness and solemnity in the woods, and the sense of loneliness, began to tell upon the spirits of the boys.

What else can it be?

Let's go and see.

BOOM

Now I know what's happened! Somebody's drowned!

That's it. They did that last summer when Bill Turner drowned.

They shoot a cannon over the water, and that makes him come up to the top. And they take loaves of bread and put mercury in them and set them afloat. Wherever there's anybody that's drowned, they'll float right there and stop.

By jings, I wish I was over there now.

I do, too. I'd give heaps to know who it is.

Suddenly, a thought flashed through Tom's mind.

Boys, I know who's drowned – it's us!

Hurray!

Whoop!

Yee-haw!!

They felt like heroes. They were missed; they were mourned; hearts were breaking on their account; tears were being shed; and best of all, they were the talk of the whole town, and the envy of all the other boys.

It was worth being a pirate after all.

As twilight drew on, the ferry boat went back to her usual business and the skiffs disappeared. The pirates were jubilant over their new grandeur and the trouble they were causing.

By and by, Joe decided to find out what the others might think about a return to civilisation.

Say, boys, what's your thoughts about going back? Maybe not tonight, but...

Boooo.

Nooooooo, Joe.

Alright, alright.

Mutiny was laid to rest for the moment.

As the night deepened, Huck began to nod, and then to snore; Joe followed next. Tom lay motionless, watching the two intently.

Some time later, he made his way cautiously, till he was out of hearing distance. Then, he broke into a run in the direction of the river. Before leaving, he wrote a message for his mates in the sand.

A few minutes later, he was in the water. He swam upstream, but was still swept downwards faster than he had expected.

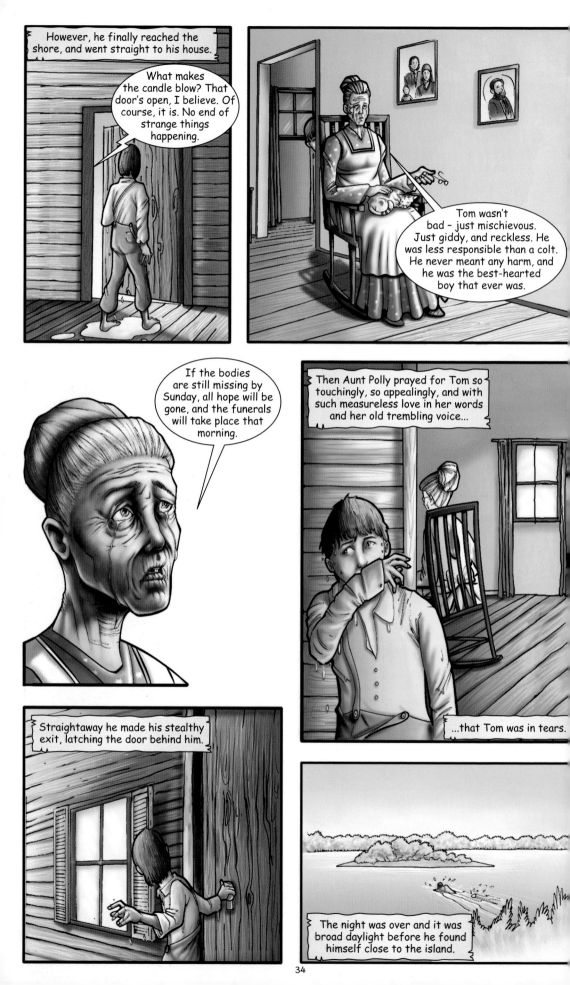

However, he finally reached the shore, and went straight to his house.

What makes the candle blow? That door's open, I believe. Of course, it is. No end of strange things happening.

Tom wasn't bad – just mischievous. Just giddy, and reckless. He was less responsible than a colt. He never meant any harm, and he was the best-hearted boy that ever was.

If the bodies are still missing by Sunday, all hope will be gone, and the funerals will take place that morning.

Then Aunt Polly prayed for Tom so touchingly, so appealingly, and with such measureless love in her words and her old trembling voice...

...that Tom was in tears.

Straightaway he made his stealthy exit, latching the door behind him.

The night was over and it was broad daylight before he found himself close to the island.

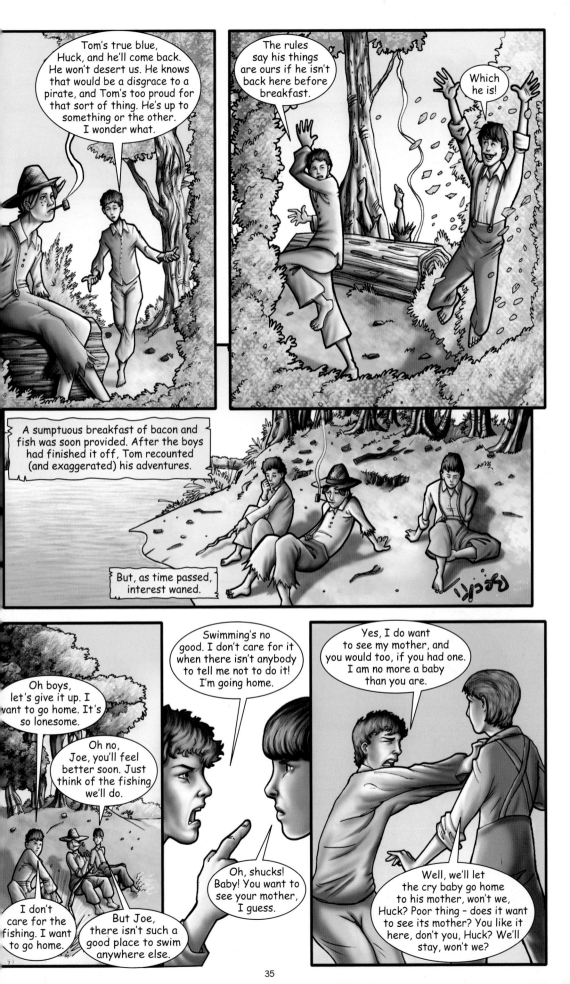

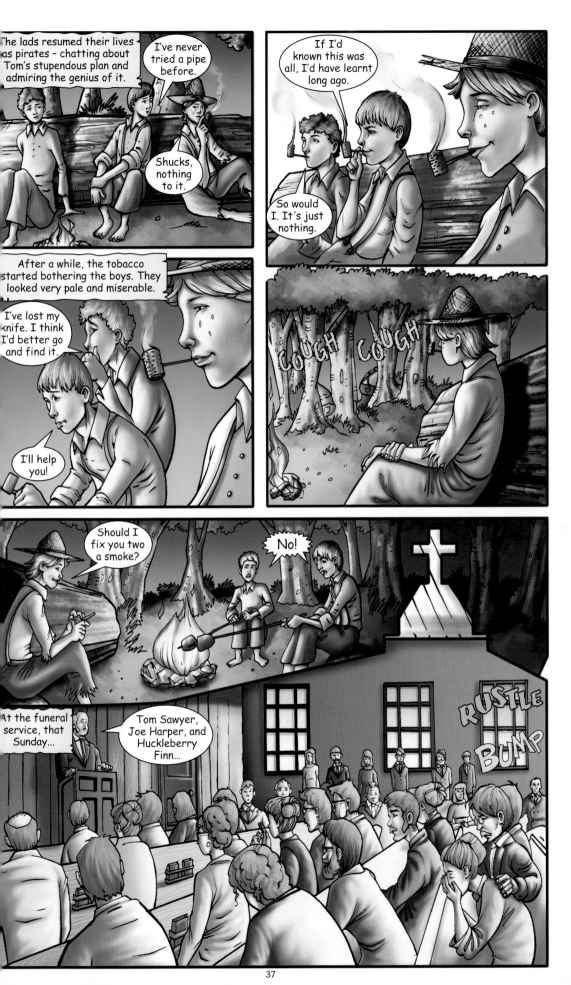

The lads resumed their lives as pirates – chatting about Tom's stupendous plan and admiring the genius of it.

I've never tried a pipe before.

Shucks, nothing to it.

If I'd known this was all, I'd have learnt long ago.

So would I. It's just nothing.

After a while, the tobacco started bothering the boys. They looked very pale and miserable.

I've lost my knife. I think I'd better go and find it.

I'll help you!

COUGH COUGH

Should I fix you two a smoke?

No!

At the funeral service, that Sunday...

Tom Sawyer, Joe Harper, and Huckleberry Finn...

RUSTLE BUMP

...I am the resurrection and I am the life...

CREEAAKK

Every pair of eyes followed the minister's. The whole congregation stared...

Good Lord!

Ahh, mercy!

...as the three dead boys came marching up the aisle. They had been hiding in the unused gallery, listening to their own funeral sermon.

Aunt Polly and the Harpers threw themselves upon their loved ones, smothered them with kisses and poured out thanksgivings.

Oh, my boy.

Joe, Joe!

Aunt Polly, it isn't fair. Somebody's got to be glad to see Huck!

Meanwhile, poor Huck stood looking uncomfortable. He didn't know what to do or where to hide from so many unwelcoming eyes.

And so they shall! I'm glad to see him, the poor motherless thing.

Praise God from whom all blessings flow. Sing everyone, and put your hearts into it.

Tom got more cuffs and kisses that day – depending on Aunt Polly's varying moods - than he'd had all year.

That was Tom's great secret – the scheme to return home with his fellow pirates and attend their own funerals!

What a hero Tom became. He did not skip and prance about. Instead, he moved with a dignified swagger, suitable to a pirate who had caught the public eye.

He pretended not to see the looks or hear the remarks as he walked along, but he enjoyed every one of them.

Then, one day, as Tom was on his way to school, he came upon Becky Thatcher.

I've acted mean, Becky, and I'm sorry. I won't ever do that again as long as I live. Please make up with me, won't you?

I'll thank you to keep to yourself, Mr Thomas Sawyer. I'll never speak to you again.

She tossed her head and walked away.

Tom was so stunned, he didn't even have the presence of mind to say 'Who cares, Miss Smarty?' until the right time to say it had gone.

But Becky did not know how fast she was nearing trouble herself.

CREAK

RRRIIIPPP

At that moment, the door opened and Tom peeped in. Becky put the book back in the drawer, tearing it in the process.

ANATOMY

Every day, Mr Dobbins, the schoolmaster, took a mysterious book out of his desk, and absorbed himself in it when the class were working in silence.

Becky found herself in the classroom. She glanced around, and the next instant she had the book in her hands.

Tom Sawyer, you are just as mean as you can be, to sneak up on a person and look at what they're looking at!

40

Gracie Miller? Susan Harper, did you do this? Rebecca Thatcher? Look me in the face!

Another denial.

Tom's uneasiness grew more and more intense under the slow torture of these proceedings. Suddenly, a thought shot like lightning through his brain. He sprang to his feet and shouted...

I did it!

The surprise, gratitude and adoration that shone out of Becky's eyes was worth a hundred floggings.

Inspired by the splendour of his own act, Tom took the most merciless flaying that Mr Dobbins had ever given, without complaint.

He also received the added cruelty of having to stay for two hours after school.

Tom, how could you be so noble?

Days passed without much happening.

But then, at last, the sleepy atmosphere in the village was vigorously stirred. The murder trial started in court. It immediately became the absorbing topic of conversation throughout the village.

Tom could not get away from it.

Well, the murder trial starts today.

Yes.

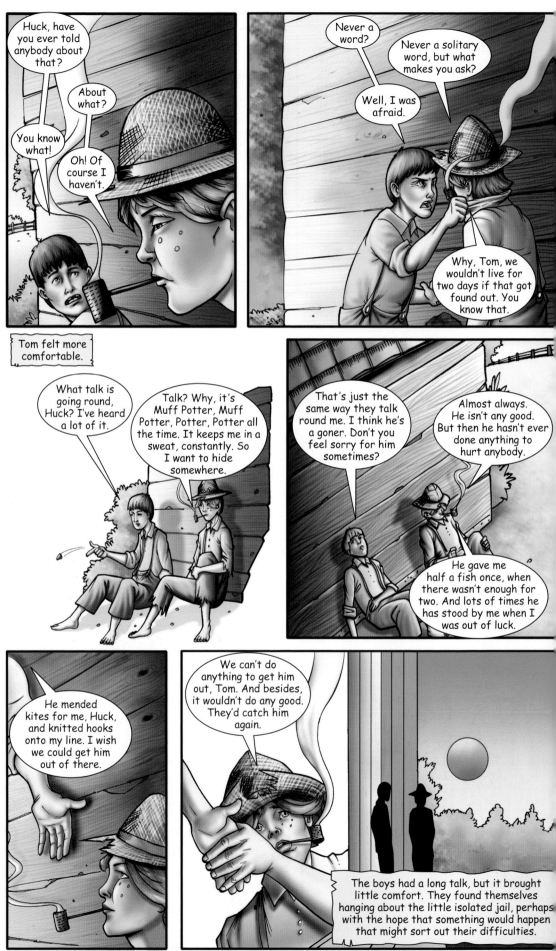

But nothing happened. There seemed to be no angels or fairies interested in this unfortunate prisoner. The boys did as they had done before – went to the cell and gave Potter some tobacco and matches.

You've been mighty good to me boys - better than anybody else in this town.

Don't you ever get drunk. Then you won't ever end up in here. Shake my hand, boys. You've helped Muff Potter and you'd help him more if you could.

Tom and Huck were speechless.

Night, Hucky.

Night, Tom.

Tom went home, miserable, and that night his dreams were full of horrors.

All the village flocked to the court the next morning, for that was to be a great day. The trial of a murderer!

What did you see, sir?

I saw him washing his hands that very morning.

44

Every eye stared at Tom as he took his place on the stand.

Thomas Sawyer, where were you on the seventeenth of June, at about the hour of midnight?

In the graveyard.

A little bit louder, please. Don't be afraid. You were--

In the graveyard!

Now, my boy, tell us everything that occurred. Tell it in your own way, but don't skip anything, and don't be afraid.

Tom began, hesitantly at first. But, as he warmed to his subject, his words flowed more and more easily.

...and then, as the doctor picked the board up and Muff Potter fell, Injun Joe jumped with the knife and--

As quick as lightning, Injun Joe sprang through the window, and was gone.

Hurrah!

Nice job, young Sawyer!

That was a brave thing to do, lad.

45

Tom was a glittering hero once more – the darling of the old, the envy of the young. His name even went into immortal print.

**VILLAGE RECORD**

T. SAWYER FREES MUFF POTTER!

During the days, Muff Potter's gratitude was enough to make Tom glad he had spoken.

But by night he wished he'd kept quiet. Half the time Tom was afraid Injun Joe would never be captured; the other half he was afraid he would be.

He was sure he would not feel safe until that man was dead and he had seen the corpse.

Rewards had been offered, and the country had been searched, but Injun Joe was not found.

One of those all-knowing and awe-inspiring marvels, a detective, came up from St Louis. He found a clue, but you can't hang a clue for murder. So, after the detective had finished and gone home, Tom felt just as insecure as before.

The slow days drifted on, and each day the fear in Tom's heart reduced.

And, in time, boyhood seemed to return to normal.

48

49

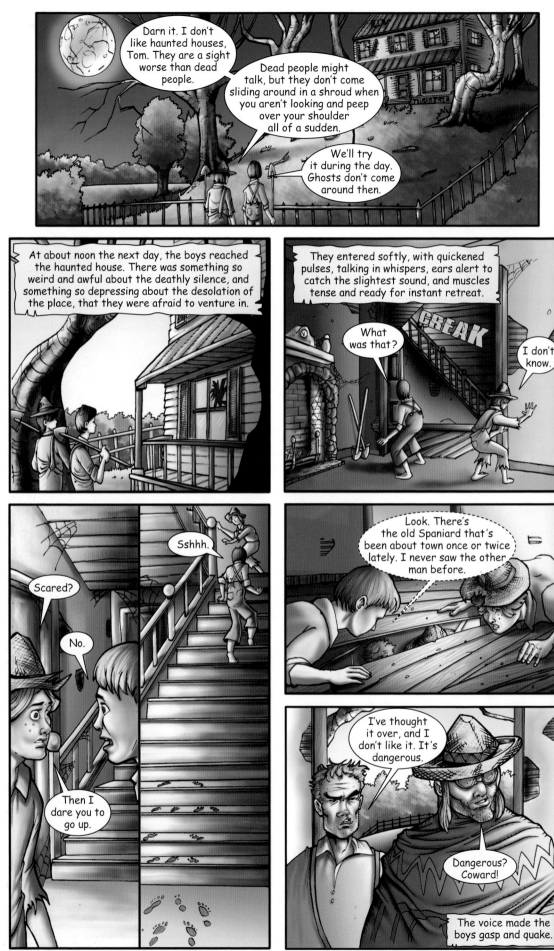

51

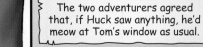

The first thing Tom heard on Friday morning was a piece of good news – Judge Thatcher's family had come back to town the night before.

...and so, Mama said I could finally have my picnic.

And you'll come, won't you, Tom Sawyer?

Hmmm.

The ferry boat was hired to take the party upstream to the picnic's location.

Those present carried out every type of activity to get them all hot and tired. Then someone shouted...

Who's ready for the caves?

Bundles of candles were produced, and straightaway everyone scampered up the hill.

The party frolicked and explored within the cave.

Eventually, one group after another came struggling back to the mouth of the cave. They were panting, laughing, smeared from head to foot with clay, and entirely delighted with the success of the day.

TING TING TING

They had been taking no note of time and were astonished to find that night had fallen. The bell of the ferry boat had been clanging for half an hour.

TINGTINGTING

Nobody cared about the wasted time, except for the captain of the craft.

Elsewhere.

Is there any use? Is there really any use in waiting round here any longer?

Suddenly, Huck heard a noise, and began paying attention immediately.

He stepped out and glided along behind the men, cat-like, with bare feet.

57

Later...

I went back to the house to look for signs, but didn't find any. I only found a bulky bundle of--

Of what?

Of burglar's tools. What's the matter with you? What were you expecting us to find?

Umm. Sunday school books, maybe.

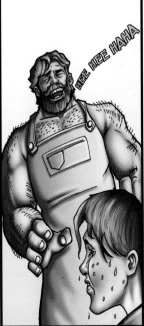

HEE HEE HAHA

Huck felt glad that they hadn't found the bundle he was thinking of. Everything seemed to be going in the right direction – the treasure must be in Number Two, Injun Joe would be captured and jailed that day, and he and Tom could seize the gold that night without any fear of interruption.

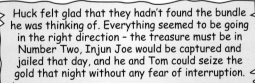

Poor old chap. You're pale and jaded. You aren't well at all, but you'll come out of it. Rest and sleep will make you better.

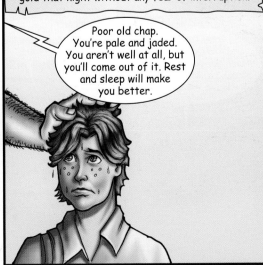

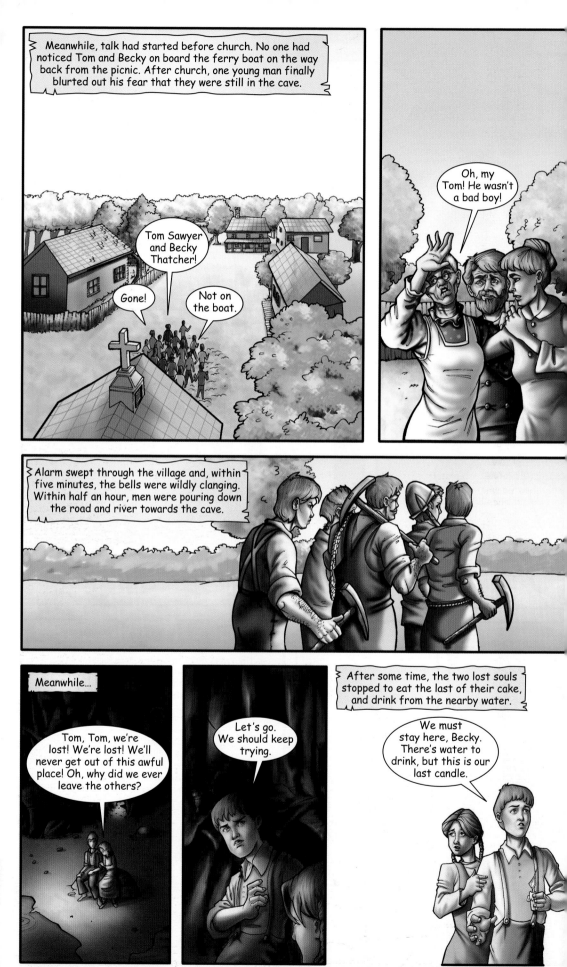

Meanwhile, talk had started before church. No one had noticed Tom and Becky on board the ferry boat on the way back from the picnic. After church, one young man finally blurted out his fear that they were still in the cave.

Tom Sawyer and Becky Thatcher!

Gone!

Not on the boat.

Oh, my Tom! He wasn't a bad boy!

Alarm swept through the village and, within five minutes, the bells were wildly clanging. Within half an hour, men were pouring down the road and river towards the cave.

Meanwhile...

Tom, Tom, we're lost! We're lost! We'll never get out of this awful place! Oh, why did we ever leave the others?

Let's go. We should keep trying.

After some time, the two lost souls stopped to eat the last of their cake, and drink from the nearby water.

We must stay here, Becky. There's water to drink, but this is our last candle.

Tom?

Yes, Becky?

Will they miss us and hunt for us!

Yes, I think they will.

Tom shouted but, in the darkness, the distant echoes sounded so hideous that he stopped.

Hey. What's this?

It's kite string. It will help me get back. I'm going to try going down some of these tunnels to find the way out.

Tom crept slowly along in the dark. Unwinding the kite string, he made an effort to stretch it as far as he could.

Tom shouted when he saw a candle, but was paralysed when he realised who he'd seen.

Injun Joe!

I'm surprised Injun Joe didn't recognise me and come to kill me for testifying in court. The echoes must have disguised my voice.

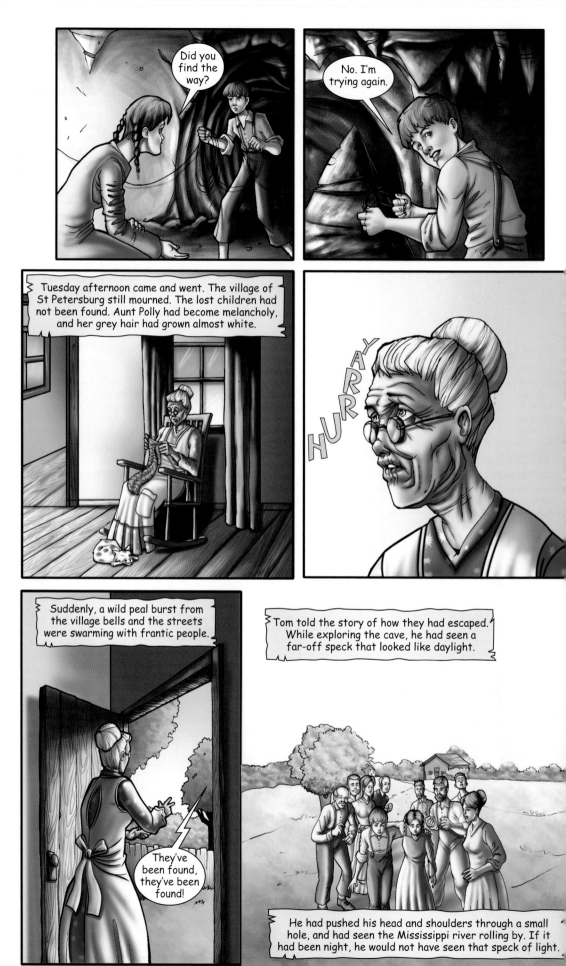

Some men had come along in a skiff and had taken them aboard. They had rowed to a house, given them supper, made them rest for two or three hours and then brought them home.

Oh, my boy! What a fright you gave me! What a fright!

Three days and nights of toil and hunger in the cave were not to be shaken off at once. Tom and Becky were bedridden all of Wednesday and Thursday, and seemed to grow more and more tired all the time.

About a fortnight after his rescue, Tom went to Judge Thatcher's house to see Becky.

Well, Tom, wouldn't you like to go to that cave again?

Yes! Yes, I would.

Well, there are others just like you, Tom. So, we have taken care of that. Nobody will get lost in that cave anymore.

Why?

Because I had its entrance covered with iron two weeks ago, and triple locked.

Tom turned as white as a sheet.

Oh no! Injun Joe was in there!

There you go, Huck. It's the snuggest hole in this country. We'll be robbers – Tom Sawyer's Gang. It sounds splendid, doesn't it, Huck?

It does, Tom. And who will we rob?

Oh, almost anybody. Waylay people – that's usually the way.

Why, it's great, Tom. It sounds better than being a pirate.

Now, where's this Number Two? Under the cross, maybe? Hey, right there's where I saw Injun Joe with his candle, Huck!

Look here, Huck. There are footprints and some candle grease on one side of the rock, but not on the other sides. Why is that? I bet you the money is under the rock. I'm going to dig in the clay.

That isn't a bad idea, Tom!

THUNK

Got it, at last! We're rich, Tom!

My goodness, Huck, look here!

Tom and Huck showed the adults the treasure, and split it half and half.

The money was counted. The sum amounted to a little over twelve thousand dollars. It was more than anyone had ever seen before.

The Widow Douglas invested Huck's money at six percent, and Judge Thatcher did the same with Tom's, at Aunt Polly's request. Each lad had an income, now, that was simply prodigious – a dollar for every weekday in the year.

Tom's and Huck's windfall caused a mighty stir in the poor little village of St Petersburg. Such a vast sum in cash seemed incredible. It was talked about, gloated over and glorified. Wherever Tom and Huck appeared they were admired and stared at.

So ends this chronicle. As it's the history of a boy, it must stop here. The story could not go much further without becoming the history of a man.

When one writes a novel about grown people, he knows exactly where to stop – with a marriage. But when he writes of boys, he must stop in the best place he can.

**CAMPFIRE™**

## About Us

It is night-time in the forest. The sky is black, studded with countless stars. A campfire is crackling, and the storytelling has begun. Stories about love and wisdom, conflict and power, dreams and identity, courage and adventure, survival against all odds, and hope against all hope – they have all come to the fore in a stream of words, gestures, song and dance. The warm, cheerful radiance of the campfire has awoken the storyteller in all those present. Even the trees and the earth and the animals of the forest seem to have fallen silent, captivated, bewitched.

Inspired by this enduring relationship between a campfire and the stories it evokes, we began publishing under the Campfire imprint in 2008, with the vision of creating graphic novels of the finest quality to entertain and educate our readers. Our writers, editors, artists and colourists share a deep passion for good stories and the art of storytelling, so our books are well researched, beautifully illustrated and wonderfully written to create a most enjoyable reading experience.

Our graphic novels are presently being published in four exciting categories. The *Classics* category showcases popular and timeless literature, which has been faithfully adapted for today's readers. While these adaptations retain the flavour of the era, they encourage our readers to delve into the literary world with the aid of authentic graphics and simplified language. Titles in the *Originals* category feature imaginative new characters and intriguing plots, and will be highly anticipated and appreciated by lovers of fiction. Our *Mythology* titles tap into the vast library of epics, myths, and legends from India and abroad, not just presenting tales from time immemorial, but also addressing their modern-day relevance. And our *Biography* titles explore the life and times of eminent personalities from around the world, in a manner that is both inspirational and personal.

Crafted by a new generation of talented artists and writers, all our graphic novels boast cutting-edge artwork, an engaging narrative, and have universal and lasting appeal.

Whether you are an avid reader or an occasional one, we hope you will gather around our campfire and let us draw you into our fascinating world of storytelling.

# ntriguing slands

## GUNKANJIMA: THE GHOST ISLAND OF JAPAN

Once an island bustling with activity and people, Gunkanjima now lies totally abandoned with crumbling streets and empty buildings. This island was famous for its coal mines during the 19th century. But when petroleum began replacing coal in the 1960s, the mines shut down and the people left the island. Today, even visitors to the island are forbidden. A very interesting fact is that Japan's first large concrete building was built on this island in 1916 – a block of apartments to house the workers of the mine.

• The English translation of the name Gunkanjima is Battleship Island; so called because of the island's resemblance to a battleship.

## BISHOP ROCK

Bishop Rock is a small island in Britain. It has been listed as the smallest island in the world with a building, in the *Guinness World Records* book. It is only 46 metres long and 16 metres wide, and has a lighthouse on it which was built in 1858. Its light is automatically operated and nobody lives on the island. Since the island has no space for anything else besides the lighthouse, a helipad has been constructed on top of the structure for easier access.

• It is believed that, in the 13th century, convicts who committed grave crimes were dispatched to the rock, with only bread and water, and left to the mercy of the waves.

**DID YOU KNOW?**
Islomania is an irresistible attraction to islands.
Authors such as Robert Louis Stevenson,
Jules Verne, Jack London and Joseph Conrad
were some famous islomaniacs!

## EASTER ISLAND

On Easter Sunday in 1722, a Dutch sailor, Jacob Roggeveen, and his crew landed on an unknown island in the Pacific close to Chile. They were stunned to find over 1,000 massive stone statues scattered all over the island, and about 2,000 people inhabiting it. Roggeveen called it Easter Island. It is believed that about 1,200 years ago, travellers came and settled on this island and carved the 'moai' out of volcanic rocks. The moai were gigantic statues of men, some as tall as a three-storeyed building. It is said that the entire population of the island was wiped out in the 1800s. What happened to them is still a mystery.

• Easter Island has an airstrip for the emergency landing of NASA space shuttles!

## ALCATRAZ, OR THE PRISON ISLAND

Alcatraz is located in San Francisco Bay, in the USA. It was named 'La Isla de los Alcatraces', which means 'Island of the Pelicans' by Spanish explorer, Juan de Ayala, in 1775. Popularly known as the 'Rock', it was most famous as a maximum security prison. The freezing waters and strong currents made it almost impossible for anyone to swim to the mainland. It closed down in 1934, and is now a very popular tourist spot.

•   Al Capone, a famous Italian-American gangster, spent time in the prison in the 1930s. He used to play his banjo in the shower room during his days there. It is said that, since his death in 1947, people have heard the sound of a banjo coming from the empty shower rooms!

## THE WORLD ISLANDS AND THE PALM ISLANDS

If you fly over the waters of the Persian Gulf, close to Dubai in the UAE, and look down, you will see a very strange sight – a map of the world and two flattened palm trees on the water! If you go closer, you'll see they are, in fact, man-made islands positioned to create these shapes. All these artificial islands are made of sand dragged from the bottom of the sea. The Palm Islands consist of three pieces of land in the shape of palm trees, while the World Islands consist of 300 islands laid out in the shape of a map of the world!

•   There are plans to build 'The Universe', a set of artificial islands in the shape of the solar system, close to the World Islands.

**DID YOU KNOW?**
Australia is a continent, and a country, as well as an island! It is often called the island continent.